To Clay and Louisa
—RTM

To Noa, who has no
trouble falling asleep
—LP

SHEEP 101

99.

By Richard T. Morris

Illustrated by LeUyen Pham

LB

LITTLE, BROWN AND COMPANY

NEW YORK   BOSTON

You guys aren't supposed
to talk to each other,
you know.

But you're a cow!

Yeah, they ran out of sheep, so they called me up.

I usually jump over the moon, so this fence thing should be a breeze.

103.

Stop right there,
pig!

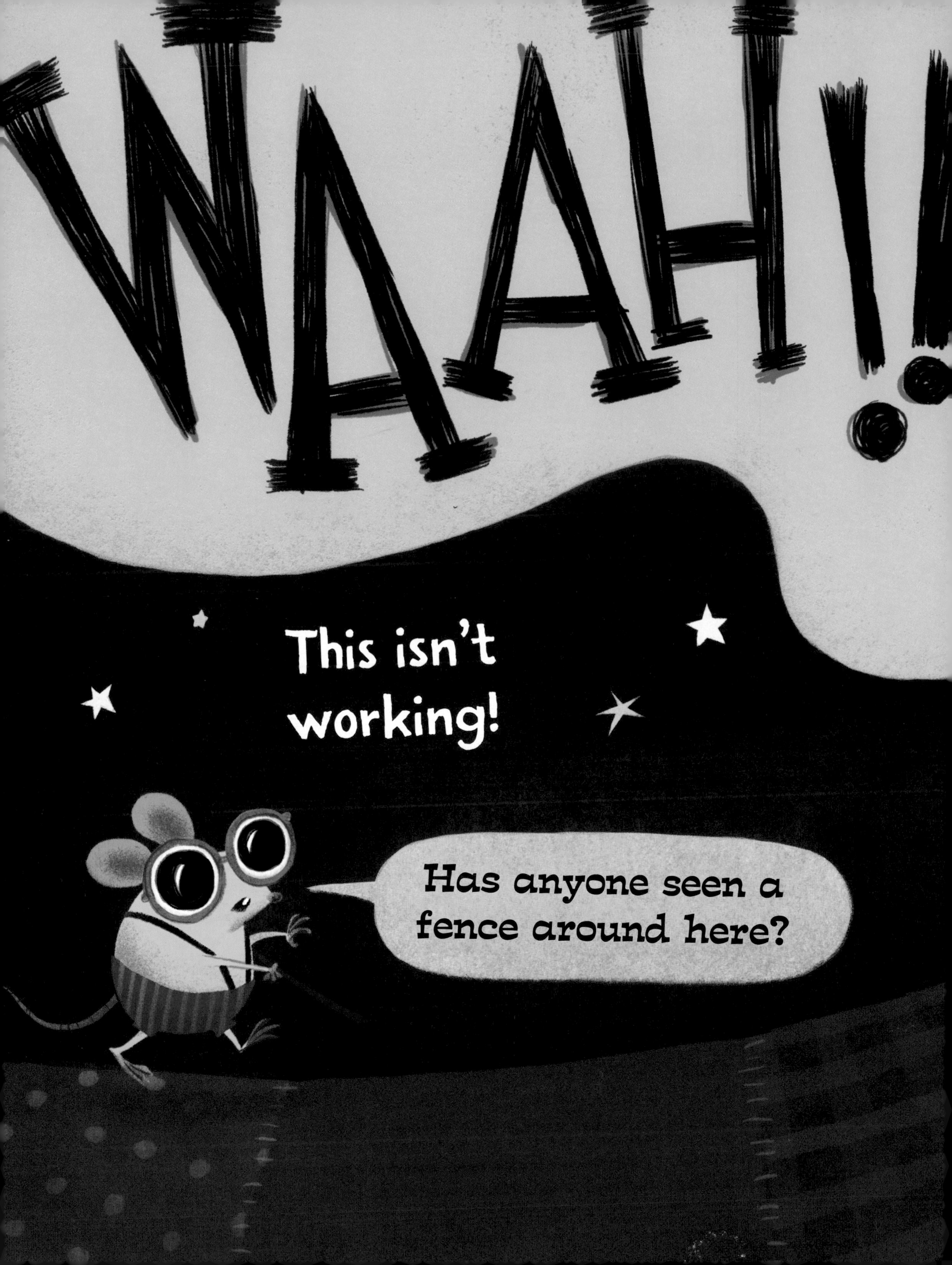
WAAH!!
This isn't working!
Has anyone seen a fence around here?

Don't tell me you're supposed to be Sheep 104.

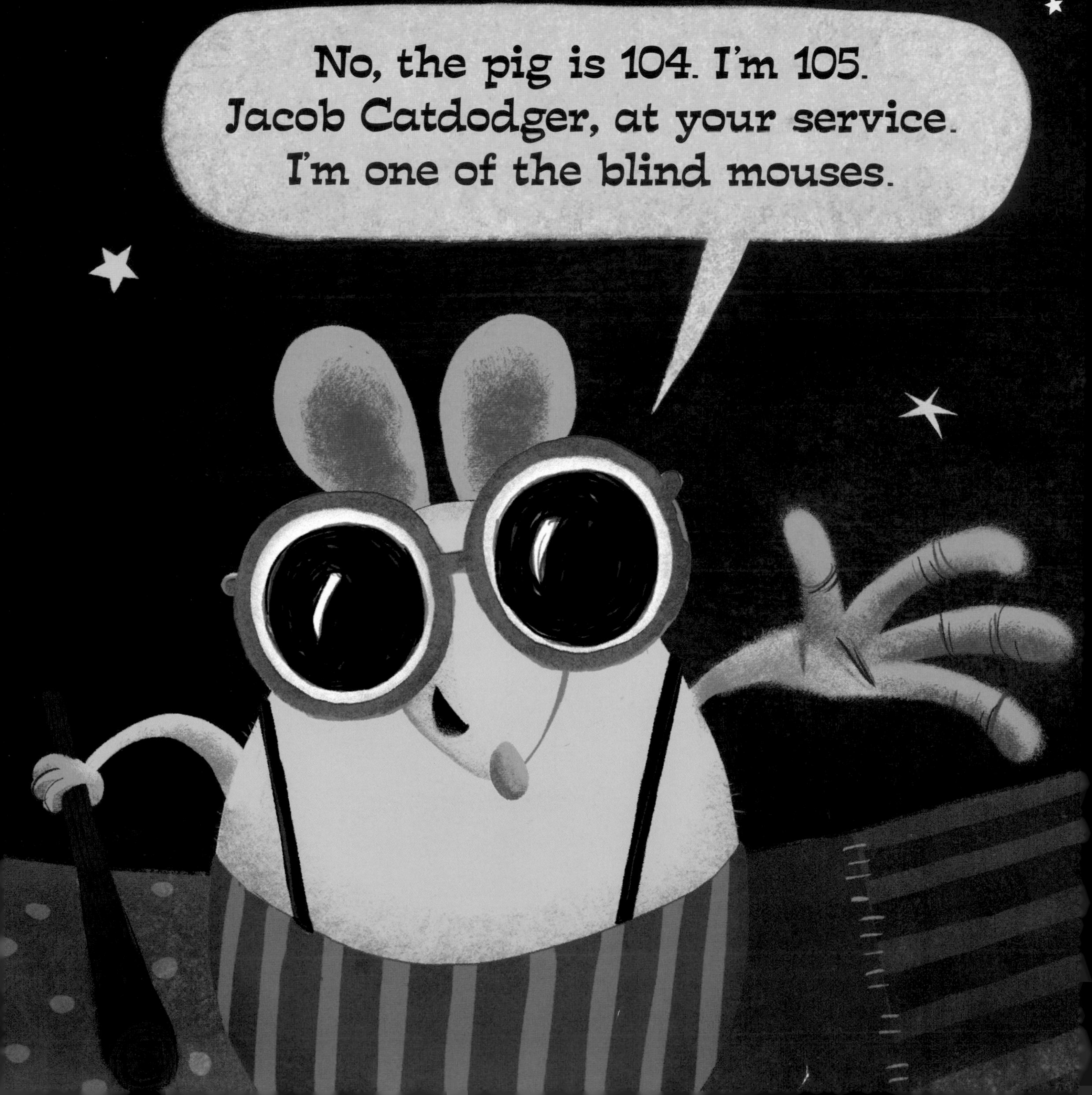

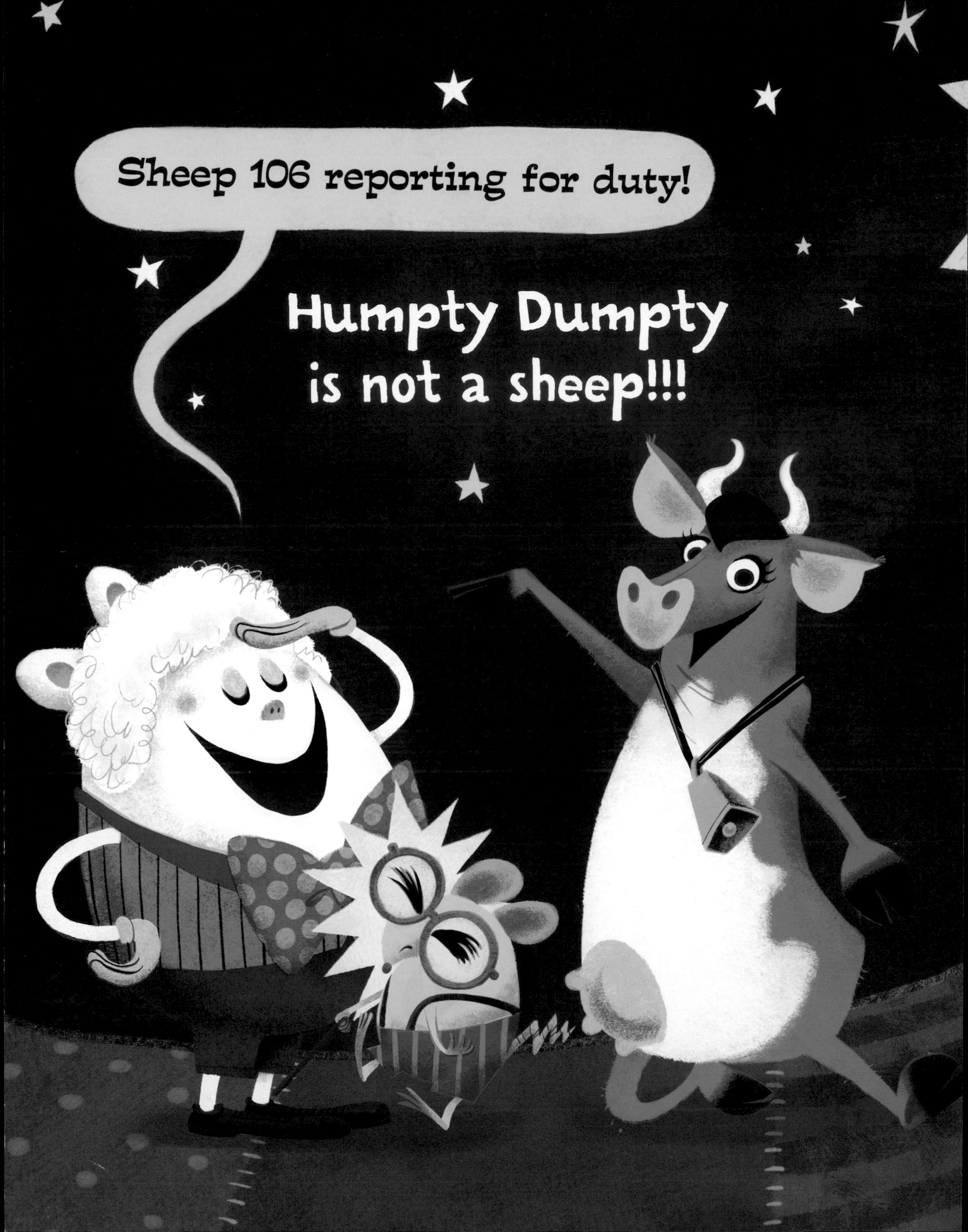

Humpty Dumpty
is not a sheep!!!

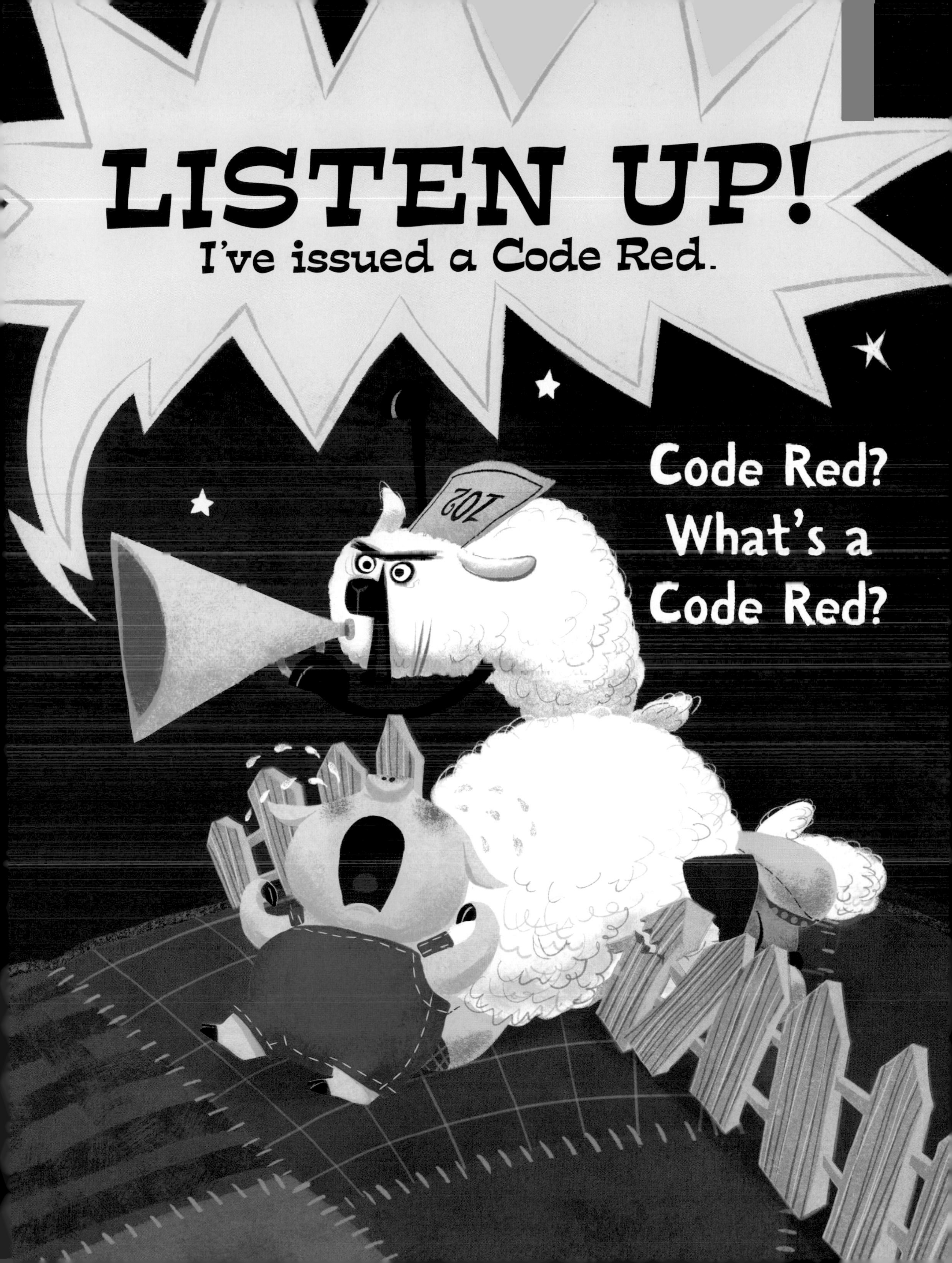
LISTEN UP!
I've issued a Code Red.
Code Red? What's a Code Red?
202

MPA-WHUMPA-
Uh, Land of Nod, this is Sandman, over. We have a visual on 101.

HUMPA-WHUMPA-W
He's stuck in there pretty good.
It looks like we're going to have to take the fence down.

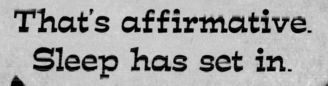

That's affirmative.
Sleep has set in.

Text copyright © 2018 by Richard T. Morris • Illustrations copyright © 2018 by LeUyen Pham • Cover illustration © 2018 by LeUyen Pham. Cover design by LeUyen Pham and Ariana Abud. Cover copyright © 2018 by Hachette Book Group, Inc. • Hachette Book Group supports the right to free expression and the value of copyright. The purpose of copyright is to encourage writers and artists to produce the creative works that enrich our culture. • The scanning, uploading, and distribution of this book without permission is a theft of the author's intellectual property. If you would like permission to use material from the book (other than for review purposes), please contact permissions@hbgusa.com. Thank you for your support of the author's rights.• Little, Brown and Company • Hachette Book Group • 1290 Avenue of the Americas, New York, NY 10104 • Visit us at LBYR.com • First Edition: March 2018 • Little, Brown and Company is a division of Hachette Book Group, Inc. The Little, Brown name and logo are trademarks of Hachette Book Group, Inc. • The publisher is not responsible for websites (or their content) that are not owned by the publisher. • Library of Congress Cataloging-in-Publication Data • Names: Morris, Richard T., 1969– author. | Pham, LeUyen, illustrator. • Title: Sheep 101 / by Richard T. Morris ; illustrated by LeUyen Pham. • Other titles: Sheep one oh one | Sheep one hundred and one • Description: New York ; Boston : Little, Brown and Company, [2018] | Summary: One hundred sheep have leapt over a fence to help a child fall asleep, but when the 101st sheep gets stuck, chaos ensues. • Identifiers: LCCN 2016044746 | ISBN 9780316213592 (hardcover) • Subjects: | CYAC: Sheep—Fiction. | Bedtime—Fiction. | Humorous stories. • Classification: LCC PZ7.M82862 She 2018 | DDC [E]—dc23 • LC record available at https://lccn.loc.gov/2016044746 • ISBNs: 978-0-316-21359-2 (hardcover), 978-0-316-47772-7 (ebook), 978-0-316-47781-9 (ebook), 978-0-316-47771-0 (ebook) • PRINTED IN CHINA • 1010 • 10 9 8 7 6 5 4 3 2 1

The illustrations for this book were rendered in crayon and pencil and completed in Adobe Photoshop. This book was edited by Alvina Ling and Nikki Garcia and designed by LeUyen Pham and Ariana Abud with art direction by Saho Fujii and Jen Keenan. The production was supervised by Virginia Lawther, and the production editor was Jen Graham. The text was set in Handy Sans, and the display type is Estro MN.